DA Alien Sports TV

by Jonny Zucker
Illustrated by Peter Richardson

Titles in Ignite

Alien Sports TV	Jonny Zucker
Monster Diner	Danny Pearson
Team Games	Melanie Joyce
Mutant Baby Werewolf	Richard Taylor
Rocket Dog	Lynda Gore
The Old Lift	Alison Hawes
Spiders from Space	Stan Cullimore
Gone Viral	Mike Gould
The Ghost Train	Roger Hurn
Dog Diaries	Clare Lawrence

Badger Publishing Limited
Oldmedow Road, Hardwick Industrial Estate,
King's Lynn PE30 4JJ
Telephone: 01438 791037

www.badgerlearning.co.uk

4 6 8 10 9 7 5 3

Alien Sports TV ISBN 978 1 84926 951 3

First edition © 2012
This second edition © 2014

Text © Jonny Zucker 2012
Complete work © Badger Publishing Limited 2012

Publisher: Susan Ross
Senior Editor: Danny Pearson
Designer: Fiona Grant
Illustrator: Peter Richardson

Alien Sports TV

Contents

Vocabulary:

strange

muttering

whacking

underneath

miserably

sheepish

Main characters:

Tom

Tara

Fring   Clob

Chapter 1

Arrival Earth

At 5 p.m. on a Monday afternoon, the aliens arrived.

They came in a large silver spaceship and landed in the park behind Tom and Tara's house.

Tom and Tara saw the lights and heard the roar of the spaceship's engine.

They ran to the park to see what was going on.

There was already a small crowd of people there.

Standing on the steps of the spaceship were two aliens, one male, one female.

They had large purple heads and thin yellow bodies covered in fur.

"Unreal," whispered Tom.

More and more people were arriving by the second.

By 7 p.m., there were hundreds of TV crews and newspaper people there.

At 7.15 p.m., the aliens suddenly held up their seven-fingered hands and the crowd went silent.

"Greetings!" announced the male alien "My name is Fring."

"And I'm Clob," said the female one.

"Don't look so alarmed," smiled Fring. "We come in peace from the planet Asta 17."

"Why have you come here?" shouted someone from the crowd.

"We are mad sports fans," said Fring.

"We want to make a TV programme that shows you humans all about our alien sports," said Clob.

"Amazing!" grinned Tara.

"Hang on a second," said Tom. "What if they're lying?"

"You heard what they said," replied Tara, "they've just come here to talk about their sports."

But Tom felt uneasy.

A few minutes later, a long limo pulled up outside the park.

A woman in a silver coat got out. "I would love to have your show on my TV station," she cried.

Fring and Clob ran over and dived into the limo. The doors closed and they sped off down the street.

Chapter 2

Alien games

"This is AMAZING!" cried Tara, pointing at the TV screen the next morning.

Fring and Clob were on the screen throwing massive blocks of ice at each other.

"This alien sport is called Freeze Power," explained Fring, as he jumped out of the way of a huge block.

"It's very popular on planet Asta," added Clob, breaking an ice pack with a kung-fu chop. "The player who gets hit the most is the loser!"

Next up, Fring and Clob played a game called Swift Cut. In this, you had to try and cut your opponent's hair while spinning round on top of ladders with wheels.

"Aren't they great?" laughed Tara.

Tom shrugged his shoulders. "I think there's more to them than we can see," he said.

"Don't be such a grump!" cried Tara. "They're just here to have fun and show us all sorts of stuff from their planet."

That night, the front page of the paper had a big photo of Fring and Clob meeting the Prime Minister.

He was trying his hand at Gargoo – a sport in which you had to eat as many strange blue, smoky sausages as you could in a minute.

"I don't like it," shivered Tom.

Tara rolled her eyes. "Everyone loves them," she said.

But Tom walked away, muttering under his breath.

Chapter 3

The great offer

The next day in PE, Tom's teacher, Mr Short, cancelled the football lesson and played an alien game called Kull-Kull instead.

This involved two teams of players crawling around the gym on their bellies, pushing a large marble with their noses into tiny goals.

"This is stupid!" hissed Tom.

After school, Tara and Tom went into Jimmy's Cafe. There was a TV on the wall.

It was showing Fring and Clob chasing each other on bendy stilts, whacking each other with huge yellow bats.

When this game finished, Clob faced the camera. "Now you have seen lots of OUR sports, we feel it's time to help YOU!" she smiled.

"That's right," nodded Fring. "We are going to give you human sportspeople some extra help."

Clob held a sparkling red T-shirt up at the camera. "This is called a Zazz Shirt," she said. "It gives you loads of sporting energy and power!"

Fring pulled a Zazz Shirt on and, a second later, he was jumping up to the ceiling of the TV studio.

"Cool!" cried Tara.

"If you want one," said Clob, "come over to the park where our spaceship is, tomorrow morning at 9 a.m."

"We will check out your size and then give you a Zazz Shirt," said Fring.

"And guess what?" grinned Clob. "They're FREE!"

"I WANT ONE!" shouted lots of people in the cafe.

"I told you they were up to something," said Tom.

"Relax!" laughed Tara, "They're only giving out free T-shirts to help us."

"I say we check this out tomorrow morning," said Tom.

"If it shuts you up, then count me in," replied Tara.

Chapter 4

Break in

"Get up!" hissed Tom.

Tara turned over in her bed and checked her clock. "It's 6 a.m.!" she said.

"We're going to check out the spaceship and the Zazz Shirts, remember?" said Tom.

Tara grumbled, but after eating some toast she felt a bit less grumpy.

Tom grabbed a ladder and they hurried down the empty street.

In the park, a fence had been put up around the spaceship.

Tom set up the ladder and they climbed over the fence.

"I can't see anything inside," said Tara, pressing her face against the dark glass. "Let's go home and get our Zazz Shirts later."

"No way!" snapped Tom. He walked round the whole spaceship and then got down on his knees.

"Look!" he whispered. "There's a small hatch underneath it. I reckon we can get in that way."

"OK," nodded Tara, "but we only go in for a minute, have a quick look and get out."

"Fine," nodded Tom.

They crawled under the ship and made it through the hatch.

"Wow!" said Tara, looking at the hundreds of blinking green and black buttons and dials inside the spaceship.

"Hey, check this out!" cried Tom.

He was pointing at a huge stack of Zazz Shirts. They were next to a large dome that said POWER DRAIN.

"I get it!" cried Tom.

"What's up?" asked Tara.

"Their plan is not about helping humans at all!" hissed Tom.

At that second, the door of the spaceship flew open. Fring and Clob walked in.

"Hi guys!" grinned Tara. "Tom has got this stupid idea that you two are up to something bad and that you are..."

"Shut it!" snapped Fring, pulling out a silver laser gun and pointing it at Tara.

"Hang on!" shouted Tara.

Clob pulled out another laser gun and pointed it at Tom.

"I TOLD YOU THEY WERE EVIL!" shouted Tom.

"BE SILENT!" snapped Fring. "You will not speak another word until all humans have been given their Zazz Shirts."

"Or else you will fry!" added Clob. "Got it?"

Tom and Tara nodded miserably.

Chapter 5

Power drain

At 7 a.m. people began to arrive in the park. They all wanted a Zazz Shirt to give them extra sports energy and power.

By 9 a.m., the line of people stretched for miles.

"OK," said Fring to Clob. "You keep your eye on these two. I'll go out and start handing out the shirts."

But as Fring walked towards the door, Tara leapt forward and hit the spaceship's LAUNCH button.

Tom jumped at Fring and Clob and kicked their guns onto the floor.

The spaceship's engine roared into life.

"GET OUT!" yelled Tara.

She and Tom jumped through the door, dragging Fring and Clob with them.

A second later, the spaceship shot into the sky.

"NOOOO!" screamed Clob. "We will never be able to get home now!"

"WHAT'S GOING ON?" yelled people in the line.

"Stay there!" Tara shouted at Fring and Clob, who were looking very sheepish.

Tara and Tom climbed on top of a high wall so that everyone in the park could see them.

Tara was holding the POWER DRAIN dome she'd grabbed from inside the ship. Tom was holding a Zazz Shirt.

"Fring and Clob weren't going to help you!" shouted Tara.

"They were going to drain your energy and take it back to their planet!" added Tom.

"No way!" shouted lots of people.

"Look!" said Tom.

He put on the Zazz Shirt. Five seconds later he suddenly went pale and started falling over. Tara grabbed him and pulled off the shirt.

"They LIED to us!" people screamed.

Everyone looked at the aliens with disgust and started walking away.

Tara and Tom jumped down from the wall and faced Fring and Clob, who looked very guilty.

"What will we do here?" groaned Fring.

"How will we get human money?" sobbed Clob.

"Don't worry," said Tom, "we'll get you a job."

"Do you have to move quickly in it?" asked Clob, hopefully.

"Oh yes!" laughed Tom.

Sports

The most popular sport in the world is football. With over 3.5 billion fans over the globe, half of the world's entire population watch or play the game.

One of the fastest-growing indoor sports is indoor sky-diving. It's great fun, but you normally only get a few minutes at a time inside the wind tunnel.

Over one billion people watch the Olympics when it is staged, every four years.

The BBC's London 2012 Olympics coverage was watched by 90% of the UK's population.

One of the oldest people ever to take part in a professional sporting event was James Hylton, who raced in an American Nascar driving race at the age of 72.

One of the world's fastest-growing sports is lacrosse. Lacrosse is a game where the players hold sticks with baskets at the end and use them to throw a ball around. It is fast moving and you need to avoid being whacked by one of the sticks.

Questions

How were Tara and Tom alerted about the spaceship's landing?

How long did it take for all of the TV crews and newspaper people to arrive?

In what way did Mr Short change his PE lesson?

Why did the Zazz Shirts sound so good?

What did Tara do to give Tom time to kick the aliens' guns away?

What would you do if aliens landed in your local park?